For Bear, from Bird – G.M.

EGMONT
We bring stories to life

First published in Great Britain 2012
by Egmont UK Limited
239 Kensington High Street, London W8 6SA

www.egmont.co.uk

Text and illustrations copyright © Gwen Millward 2012
Gwen Millward has asserted her moral rights

ISBN 978 1 4052 5426 7 (Hardback)
ISBN 978 1 4052 5427 4 (Paperback)

1 3 5 7 9 10 8 6 4 2

A CIP catalogue record for this title
is available from the British Library

Printed and bound in Singapore

46303/1/2

# Bear
and
Bird

## Gwen Millward

EGMONT

Bear and Bird were best friends.

They lived together in a house *B*ear had made for them, in the middle of a beautiful forest.

Every day, *B*ear and *B*ird
went into the forest to collect wood
for their fire, and to gather berries
and bugs for their supper.

While Bear worked hard looking after Bird, cooking him his favourite birch-twig and rose-hip soup . . .

. . . Bird sang his favourite songs.

Winter was coming and wise Owl
warned all forest creatures that
it was going to be very cold.

He told them to gather enough
firewood and food to last until spring.

So *Bear* and *Bird* collected
as much wood and food
as they could carry.

One very cold evening,
Bird put ALL the wood
they had gathered on to the fire.

There was none left.

*B*ear gave a deep sigh and went out into the snowy night to get some more.

Hours went by and *B*ear had not returned.

*B*ird began to worry.

Bird had to be brave.

He put on his warmest hat and scarf,
and went to look for Bear.

Bird followed Bear's paw prints in the snow.

Suddenly, Fox came running through the trees.
"Have you seen *Bear*?" asked *Bird*.

"No," said Fox. "Sorry, I can't stop. I'm on my way to help Weasel.
She has a hole in her roof that's letting in snow."

And she hurried away.

Bird thought to himself,
"What a lovely thing for Fox to do."

He thought of all the wonderful
things Bear did for him.

Bear's paw prints were
beginning to disappear in the snow.

Just then, Squirrel scurried down a tree.

"Have you seen *Bear*?" asked *Bird*.

"No," said Squirrel. "Sorry, I can't stop.
Badger's out of food, so I'm taking him some of my nuts."

"That's a good friend," thought *Bird*. "What a lovely thing to do for Badger."
And he continued on his way.

Bear's paw prints came to a
sudden end at the bottom of a tree.

"I should have done more
to help Bear," sobbed Bird.

Just then, he heard a sound from above.

Bird
shone his
torch up
into the
tree.

"Bear!"

Bird sang with joy.

Bear was afraid and shivering with cold.
He had got lost and couldn't find his way home in the dark.

Bird helped Bear down from the tree
and gave him a BIG warm hug.

Then
the two friends
walked home together,
collecting firewood on the way.

When at last they arrived
at their snow-covered house,
*B*ird wrapped *B*ear
in a warm blanket . . .

built a toasty fire . . .

. . . and made them both a steaming cup of hot chocolate.

From then on,
Bird always helped Bear
to collect wood for the fire,
and to gather berries and bugs
for their supper.

And, best of all,
Bird still sang his lovely songs
while the two friends worked together.